THE BULLY OF GLENDALE POND

Written by Clyde R. Smith

Illustrated by Pauline Perin

PublishAmerica
Baltimore

First printing

Softcover 9781462677955
PUBLISHED BY PUBLISHAMERICA, LLLP
www.publishamerica.com
Baltimore

Printed in the United States of America

THE BULLY OF GLENDALE POND

There is a pond on the edge of a forest. Trees line the edge of the pond all the way around it. Now and then, a fish can be seen as it jumps out of the water to catch a fly or some other bug.

During the spring when the ice melts, ducks will land on this pond to rest for their journey to go north to their summer home. In the fall when they go back south to get out of the cold weather, they will often land on this same pond to stay for an evening's rest.

On one previous trip, the flock of ducks landed on a much bigger pond that was quite a few miles south of this one. When the ducks took off in the morning to head north again, one of the ducks accidentally paddled through a frog's nest. One of the frog eggs stuck to it's foot, and the duck rose into the air not realizing the egg was still attached to it's foot.

When the ducks landed on that little pond in the forest, the egg came loose in the water, and sank into the mud along the edge of the pond. There it lay until it hatched, and a tiny tadpole came slowly swimming to the top of the water.

This was not unusual as there were many other frogs calling this little pond home, and their eggs were also turning into little tadpoles. But the egg that rode in on the duck's foot was not a regular frog's egg. It came from a big bullfrog that lived in the pond further south where she had laid her eggs. A bullfrog can't count, so it had no idea how many little tadpoles were a son or daughter. She was not going to Miss the one tadpole that ended up further north in that little pond.

That little tadpole grew and grew until it was much bigger than any of the other tadpoles in that pond, so it ate much more than the others. It would swim around until it saw others eating on some favorite food, then barge right in, pushing them out of the way to get to the best feeding spot. There was nothing the little tadpoles could do except call him a big bully, and a hog, as he ate it all for himself.

By and by, the tadpoles all started to grow legs, and lose their tail. They were now all turning into little frogs, except for that big tadpole, who was turning into a much bigger frog. This big frog continued his bad behavior by shoving the smaller ones out of his was, and claiming the best spot on the pond bank to warm himself in the sun. All the little frogs did not like him, so refused to play with him, or even sit close to him while sunning themselves by the side of the pond.

Summertime was a good time for catching flies, and bugs to eat. One little frog jumped high into the air to catch a dragonfly. Before he had time to eat it, that big frog quickly hopped over, and demanded that it be given to him. The little frog gave up his prize, and hopped off to complain to his friends about the big bully's behavior. The big frog was quickly becoming an enemy of all the little frogs. This big bullfrog would hop up on the bank at the edge of the pond, and at the top of his voice would yell.

"I am the biggest frog in this pond, and I am the most important frog in this pond!"

Summertime gradually came to an end, and by this time all the frogs had reached their full size. They could now sit around the pond and sing their song. A chorus of high-pitched sounds filled the air around the pond, and then an ear-shattering, low sound would split the air from that big bull frog. It sounded like somebody blowing on an old tuba with a leaky valve. All the little frogs would stop their singing for a minute, in shock at that sound, before gradually beginning their song again. The big bullfrog didn't care what they thought of his noise making. He seemed to enjoy letting one big croooaaak rip through the air that scared the little ones enough to stop their singing He was just a big bully even when it came to singing.

The weather was becoming colder now. Soon there would be snow, and the pond would freeze over. All the little frogs had learned from their parents how to dig down deep into the mud for protection from the bitter freezing temperatures. But the big bully thought he was too important to be bothered to learn anything from a little frog. So he sang out with his ear-splitting loud croooaaak all by himself now.

But it was just no fun with nobody else to listen to him. It was very lonely with no other frogs to see or hear. The days were getting cold now, and he was close to freezing. The bitter cold was painful. He could hardly move, and when he tried to croak a song he could hardly make a sound. Wondering where everyone else had gone, he slowly swam around the pond looking for the other little frogs. He was one sad bullfrog as he sat on a rock all by himself.

He finally came upon one wise old little frog still in the pond. "Where is everybody?" he asked the old frog.

The old frog explained how they had all dug down into the mud for protection from the winter cold, and he was going to do the same thing now. He had only remained this long to see that all the others were saftely dug in.

"Why are you still here?" he asked the bull frog.

"I didn't know what I was supposed to do. Nobody told me about digging down into the mud for the winter. How do you do that?" the bullfrog asked.

"Maybe if you would be nice to the others, and not boss them around, they would have shown you how to dig into the mud. If you stay here you will freeze, and die before spring comes. Follow me, and I will show you how to do it, and help you get started." So the old frog showed him how to use his feet to dig down into the mud.

"Next spring when you wake up and come back up to the surface, you can be a much better frog. remember this. It is nice to be important, but it is a lot more important to be nice." And with that thought in his mind, both the bullfrog and the old frog went to sleep for the winter.

That next spring when they all came back to the surface, he was a different bullfrog. He greeted each one with a happy croak. Food was shared withe the small frogs. When he jumped up high to catch a big dragonfly, then gave it to a small frog. They knew he really had changed. They even showed him how to join in with his big croooaaak at the right time to make a nice sounding concert of frog songs.

It was really good to have freinds. This was much better than being a bully.

THE END